CHARLIE
AND
THE MAGIC TREE

Written By: Crystal Bass

Illustrated By: Mehk Arshad

CHARLIE
AND
THE MAGIC TREE

By
Crystal Bass

Published by Clarice Jefferies Publishing

Contact info: cjpublishing@yahoo.com

For permissions, contact: cjpublishing@yahoo.com

Printed in the United States of America on responsibly sourced paper

My Daughters
Mom Loves You

My Nieces and Nephews
Auntie Loves You

My Younger Brother
I Love You

My Younger Sister
I Love and Miss You

One Saturday morning, Charlie woke up, and her dog Teddy, was waiting for her when she got out of bed. Teddy was very happy to see her. He was wagging his tail, jumping up and down, waiting for his attention. After giving Teddy his hugs and kisses, Charlie looked out of her bedroom window and saw her favorite tree across the street at the park. She waved and said, "Good morning, my favorite tree."

Charlie could also see her friends playing and having a great time at the park. Charlie's father was at work, so she asked her mother if she could go to the park and play with her friends. Charlie's mom said, "Of course you can, have fun and be safe." Charlie got dressed as fast as she could and ran across the street to the park.

When Charlie got to the park, she said hi to her friends: Corey, Judy, Maria, and Keysha. They were happy to see Charlie and began to play many different games. The first game they played was tag. They had a lot of fun running around, laughing, giggling, and chasing each other.

Next, they played on the swings. They had a lot of fun taking turns pushing each other as they swung as high as they could. Then, they played on the slide. They had a lot of fun taking turns climbing up the slide and racing down the slide.

Then Charlie shouted, "Let's play hide and seek! I will be it. I'm going to count to ten, so you all better run and hide!"
Charlie turned around and faced her favorite tree. She closed her eyes and began to count,"1 one thousand, 2 one thousand, 3 one thousand." Charlie's friends laughed and giggled as they raced around, looking for the best hiding places.

Judy and Maria hid under the slide. Keysha hid behind a big tree. And Corey hid under the picnic table.
Charlie finished counting to ten and shouted, "Ready or not, here I come!" She turned around and spotted Corey hiding under the picnic table; Corey began to run as Charlie chased him.

Judy and Maria shouted with laughter as they ran out of their hiding places. They all ran to tag the tree and yelled, "I'm safe!"
Charlie tagged Keysha, and now it was her turn to be it, so Keysha turned to face the tree, covered her eyes, and began to count to ten.

Charlie and her friends started running around searching for a good hiding place. Everyone found a good place to hide except for Charlie; she could not find a good place to hide anywhere.

Charlie looked up and said, "I wish I could climb to the top of my favorite tree. That would be the best hiding place ever."

Then, right before her very eyes, the magical tree came to life. It opened its big, beautiful, brown eyes and looked down at Charlie with such a big smile that it warmed her heart. Charlie thought, "Could my favorite tree be looking at me?"
The magical tree winked at Charlie and let down one of its big, beautiful branches. Charlie climbed onto the branch, and the tree lifted her high up, up, and into the sky!

Charlie began to see all kinds of beautiful birds of different colors - like red, yellow, brown, and blue. They were chirping, singing, and flapping their wings around her. All the bird's knew Charlie's name, and they all stopped to say hi to Charlie as they admired her beautiful skin color.

Charlie spotted a mother squirrel running around, playing and chasing her little brown babies. All the squirrels stopped playing to tell Charlie how nice it was to see her and how much they loved her beautiful natural hair. Charlie thought to herself, "What a wonderful place this is."

At this time, Keysha finished counting to ten and shouted, "Ready or not, here I come!"
Keysha spotted Judy and Corey hiding behind a big bush and began chasing after them. Maria ran to tag the magical tree. Everyone made it back to the magic tree except for Charlie.

All her friends looked at each other and asked, "Where is Charlie?"
Her friends began to look for Charlie all around the park.

They looked under the picnic table...
They looked under the slide...
They looked behind the bushes...
And they even looked behind the trees...

Charlie looked down at her friends from her hiding place and began giggling. Her friends said, "Maybe Charlie went home to hide. Let's go and check her house."

Charlie's friends began to walk across the park toward Charlie's home. Charlie told her magic tree, "Now would be a good time to put me down. I am going to surprise my friends."

The magic tree lowered Charlie down to the ground and just before Charlie's friends were about to cross the street, Charlie shouted, "Here I am!"

Charlie's friends ran back to the magical tree as fast as they could. Charlie tagged the tree and shouted, "I'm safe."

Charlie looked up at her magical tree and winked. The tree winked back at her. At this time, their mothers shouted, "Lunch is ready, it's time to come home and eat!"

Everyone raced home for lunch, but before Charlie left, she gave her magic tree a big, big hug and said, "I love you my magic tree." The tree wrapped its gigantic branches around Charlie and said, "I love you too Charlie."

Milton Keynes UK
Ingram Content Group UK Ltd.
UKHW050343071123
432102UK00003B/20